Shooting Stars Soccer Team

Written by Yeong-ah Kim

Illustrated by Hyeong-jin Lee

Edited by Joy Cowley

Zebra ran very well.
He also kicked very well.
Captain Lion saw Zebra
and said to him,
"Would you like to join
the Shooting Stars soccer team?"

"Yes, yes!" cried Zebra.
"I'd love to join!"

So Zebra became a soccer player.
Although he could kick and run,
he didn't know how to play soccer.

"Oh, who cares!" he said.
"I just have to kick the ball
into the goal. I will be fine!"

Shooting Stars
Soccer Team

4

Soon there was a game
between the Shooting Stars soccer team
and the Cyclones soccer team.

"I'll do it!" shouted Zebra.
"I'll score a goal!"

He took the ball from his
friend and ran fast with it.

6

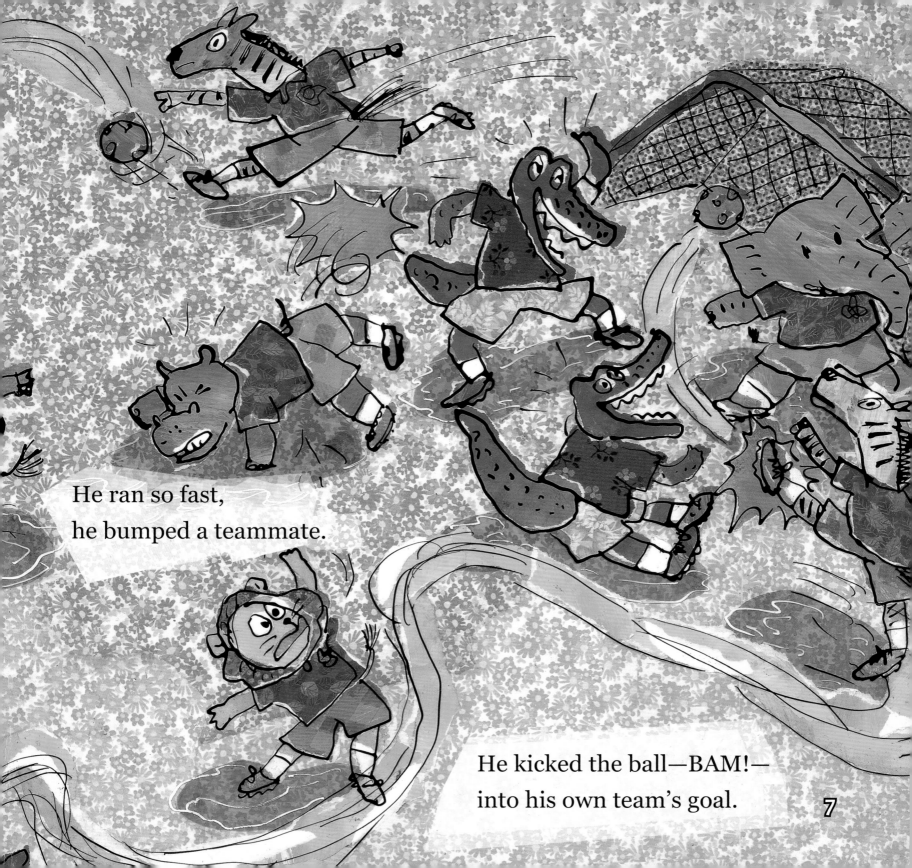

He ran so fast,
he bumped a teammate.

He kicked the ball—BAM!—
into his own team's goal.

7

The Shooting Stars soccer team lost 5 to 0.
"It's the first time we've played badly,"
one of the players said.

But Zebra was excited!
"I scored a goal!" he said.

The players were angry.

"It's Zebra's fault we lost today!"

"He wanted the ball for himself."

"He doesn't know how to play soccer."

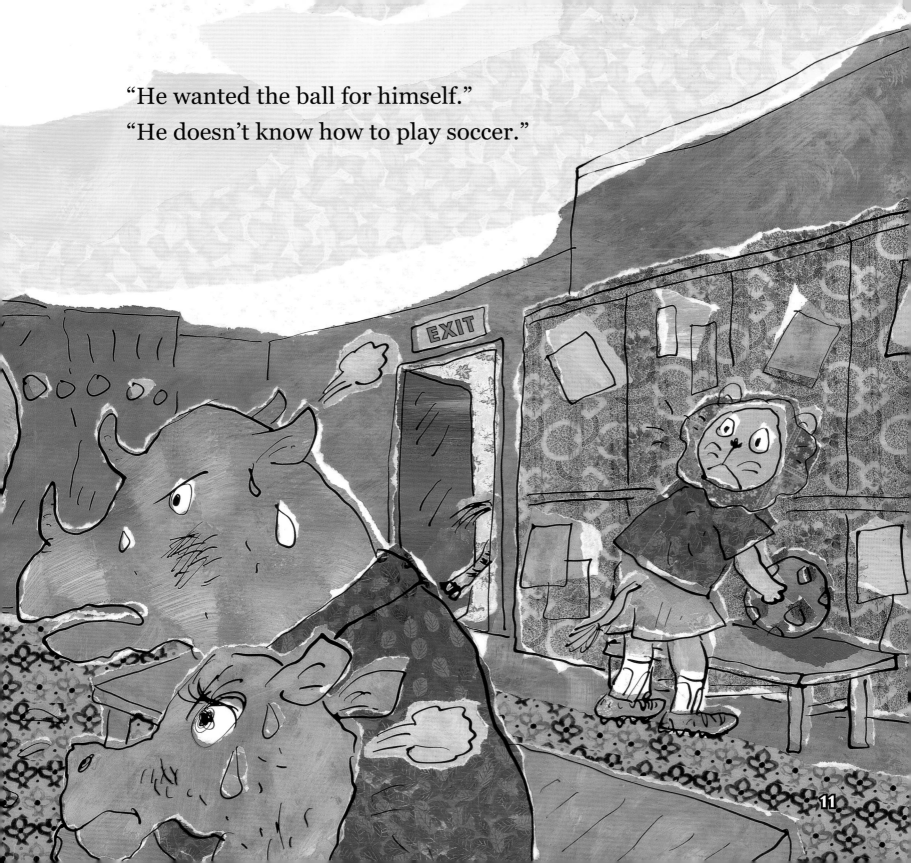

From then on,
the Shooting Stars soccer team
ignored Zebra.
They practised without him.

13

Captain Lion spoke to the players.
"Don't leave Zebra out. Talk to him.
Tell him what he did wrong."

The other players shrugged.
"Even if we told him,
would he listen to us?"

14

Captain Lion did not give up.
He made every player sit down
to watch a video of the last game.

16

"Let's see how we can play
a better game," he said
as he switched on the video.

17

When Zebra bumped his teammate,
Captain Lion said, "Zebra, you run fast,
but you shouldn't do that to your friends."

"Sorry," said Zebra, "I didn't know that."

When Zebra took the ball from his teammate,
Captain Lion said, "Soccer is played by a team.
Everyone works together on a team."

Zebra hung his head. "Sorry."

"Look at that!" said Captain Lion. "You shouldn't kick the ball into your own team's goal."

Zebra was very embarrassed.
"Now I know why you are angry.
I suppose you don't want me
on the Shooting Stars team."

21

The players gathered around Zebra.
"What are you saying?
We all belong on the team.
Let's give it one more try."

"Oh, thank you!" said Zebra.

From then on,
Zebra worked hard.

24

He ran fast and kicked the ball hard.
He also passed the ball,
and he helped his teammates
score goals.

Soon there was another match
between the Shooting Stars soccer team
and the Cyclones soccer team.

Zebra remembered Captain Lion's words.

Soccer was played by a team.

Everyone needed to work together.

BAM!

The Shooting Stars team scored a fantastic goal. It was not Zebra's goal, but he was very happy because he had helped a teammate make the point. Zebra knew what it meant to be a part of the team.

Go Team!

WIN
Shooting Stars

29

Dear Zebra,

I am so happy to have you on the Shooting Stars team.
You help us play a better game of soccer.
You have worked hard.
You learned how to help your teammates.
We all need to work together.
That's what it means to be part of a team.
I'm glad you are part of our team!

Your teammate, Captain Lion

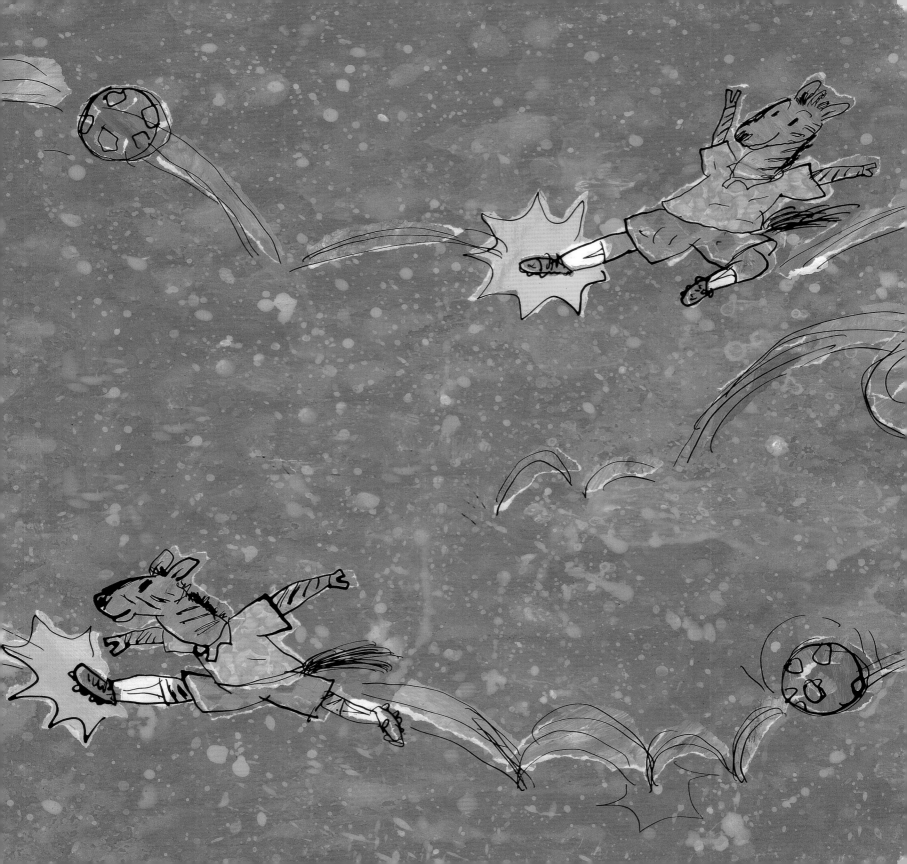

big & SMALL

Original Korean text by Yeong-ah Kim
Illustrations by Hyeong-jin Lee
Original Korean edition © Aram Publishing

This English edition published by big & SMALL
by arrangement with Aram Publishing
English text edited by Joy Cowley
Additional editing by Mary Lindeen
Artwork for this edition produced
in cooperation with Norwood House Press, U.S.A.
English edition © big & SMALL 2015

ISBN: 978-1-925233-93-3

Printed in Korea